Mr. Putter & Tabby
Pour the Tea

CYNTHIA RYLANT

Mr. Putter & Tabby Pour the Tea

Illustrated by

ARTHUR HOWARD

sandpiper

Houghton Mifflin Harcourt

Boston   New York

For Grandmama and Whiskers
—C. R.

For James Tilton
—A. H.

www.hmhco.com

First Harcourt paperback edition 1994

Library of Congress Cataloging-in-Publication Data
Rylant, Cynthia.
Mr. Putter & Tabby pour the tea/Cynthia Rylant;
illustrated by Arthur Howard.
p.   cm.
Summary: Mr. Putter gets an old cat to share his life with him.
[1. Cats—Fiction.   2. Old age—Fiction.]   I. Howard, Arthur, ill.
II. Title.   III. Title. Mr. Putter & Tabby pour the tea.
PZ7.R982Mt   1994
[E]—dc20   93-21470
ISBN 978-0-15-256255-7 hc
ISBN 978-0-15-200901-4 pb

Manufactured in China
SCP 47 46 45 44 43
4500817769

1

Mr. Putter

2

Tabby

3

Mr. Putter and Tabby

1

Mr. Putter

Before he got his fine cat, Tabby,
Mr. Putter lived all alone.

In the mornings he had no one
to share his English muffins.
In the afternoons he had no one
to share his tea.

And in the evenings
there was no one
Mr. Putter could
tell his stories to.
And he had the
most wonderful
stories to tell.

All day long as Mr. Putter
clipped his roses
and fed his tulips
and watered his trees,
Mr. Putter wished for
some company.

He had warm muffins to eat.

He had good tea to pour.

And he had wonderful stories to tell.

Mr. Putter was tired of living alone.

Mr. Putter wanted a cat.

2

Tabby

Mr. Putter went to the pet store.

"Do you have cats?" he asked the

pet store lady.

"We have fourteen," she said.

Mr. Putter was delighted.

But when he looked into the cage,

he was not.

"These are kittens," he said.

"I was hoping for a cat."

"Oh, no one wants cats, sir,"

said the pet store lady.

"They are not cute.

They are not peppy."

Mr. Putter himself had not
been cute and peppy for a
very long time.
He said, "I want a cat."

"Then go to the shelter, sir,"
said the pet store lady.
"You are sure to find a cat."

Mr. Putter went to the shelter.

"Have you any cats?"
he asked the shelter man.
"We have a fat gray one,
a thin black one,
and an old yellow one," said the man.
"Did you say old?" asked Mr. Putter.

The shelter man brought Mr. Putter
the old yellow cat.
Its bones creaked,
its fur was thinning,
and it seemed a little deaf.
Mr. Putter creaked,
his hair was thinning,
and he was a little deaf, too.

So he took the old yellow cat home.

He named her Tabby.

And that is how their life began.

3
Mr. Putter and Tabby

Tabby loved Mr. Putter's tulips.
She was old,
and beautiful things
meant more to her.

She would rub past all
the yellow tulips.
Then she would roll past
all the red tulips.

Then she would take her bath
among all the pink tulips.
Mr. Putter clipped roses
while Tabby bathed.

In the mornings
Mr. Putter and Tabby liked to share
an English muffin.
Mr. Putter ate his with jam.
Tabby ate hers with cream cheese.

In the afternoons

Mr. Putter and Tabby

liked to share tea.

Mr. Putter took his with sugar.

Tabby took hers with cream.

And in the evenings
they sat by the window,
and Mr. Putter told stories.
He told the most wonderful stories.
Each story made Tabby purr.

On summer days they warmed their
old bones together in the sun.
On fall days they took
long walks through the trees.
And on winter days they turned
the opera up *very* loud.

After a while it seemed as if
they had always lived together.
Tabby knew just what Mr. Putter
was going to do next.
Mr. Putter knew just where Tabby
was going to sleep next.

In the mornings each looked for the other as soon as they opened their eyes.

And at night each looked for
the other as their eyes were closing.
Mr. Putter could not remember
life without Tabby.

Tabby could not remember
life without Mr. Putter.
They lived among their
tulips and trees.

They ate their muffins.

They poured their tea.

They turned up the opera,

and enjoyed the most

perfect company of all —

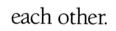

each other.

The illustrations in this book were done in pencil, watercolor,
gouache, and Sennelier pastels on 90-pound vellum paper.
The display type was set in Minya Nouvelle, Agenda, and Artcraft.
The text type was set in Berkeley Old Style Book.
Color separations by Bright Arts, Ltd., Singapore
Production supervision by Warren Wallerstein and Ginger Boyer
Series cover design by Kristine Brogno and Michele Wetherbee
Cover design by Brad Barrett
Designed by Arthur Howard and Trina Stahl